W9-BLY-810

STEP-BY-STEP EXPERIMENTS WITH INSECTS

By Katie Marsico

Illustrated by Bob Ostrom

The Child's World

Published by The Child's World®
1980 Lookout Drive • Mankato, MN 56003-1705
800-599-READ • www.childsworld.com

ACKNOWLEDGMENTS
The Child's World®: Mary Berendes, Publishing Director
The Design Lab: Design and production
Red Line Editorial: Editorial direction
Consultant: Diane Bollen, Project Coordinator, Mars Rover Mission,
    Cornell University

ISBN 9781609733391
LCCN 2011940141

PHOTO CREDITS
David Morch/Dreamstime, cover; Pilar Echeverria/Dreamstime, cover,
back cover; Vladimir Sazonov/Dreamstime, 1, 31; Karel Gallas/Shutter-
stock Images, 4; Adrian Matthiassen/Dreamstime, 5, 29; Arto Hakola/
Shutterstock Images, 8; Dreamstime, 13; Michael Wesemann/Shutter-
stock Images, 14; Shutterstock Images, 18, 20, 24

Design elements: Pilar Echeverria/Dreamstime, Robisklp/Dreamstime,
Jeffrey Van Daele/Dreamstime, Sarit Saliman/Dreamstime

Printed in the United States of America

BE SAFE !

The experiments in this book are
meant for kids to do themselves.
Sometimes an adult's help is
needed though. Look in the
supply list for each experiment.
It will list if an adult is needed.
Also, some supplies will need to
be bought by an adult.

TABLE OF CONTENTS

4

Beetles can be large insects.

CHAPTER ONE

Study Insects!

Insects fly, creep, and crawl all around us. Have you ever looked at one up close? It has six legs and an **exoskeleton**. That means its skeleton is on the outside of its body. There are three main parts of an insect's body. These parts are the head, the **thorax** in the middle, and the **abdomen** in the rear. Many insects also have wings. Not all insects fly though.

Insects come in many shapes and sizes. Some are small and round, like ladybugs. Others are as big as your hand, like some large beetles. Can you name a few kinds of insects? Bees, ants, and butterflies are insects. How can you learn more about insects?

CHAPTER TWO

Seven Science Steps

Doing a science **experiment** is a fun way to discover new facts. An experiment follows steps to find answers to science questions. This book has experiments to help you learn about insects. You will follow the same seven steps in each experiment:

Seven Steps

1. Research: Figure out the facts before you get started.

2. Question: What do you want to learn?

3. Guess: Make a **prediction**. What do you think will happen in the experiment?

4. Gather: Find the supplies you need for your experiment.

5. Experiment: Follow the directions.

6. Review: Look at the results of the experiment.

7. Conclusion: The experiment is done. Now it is time to reach a **conclusion**. Was your prediction right?

Are you ready to become a scientist? Let's experiment to learn about insects!

Ants are easy to find outside.

CHAPTER THREE

Cold-Blooded Critters

What does temperature do to insects? See what happens as the temperature around them changes.

Research the Facts

Here are a few. Can you find some more?

- Insects are **cold-blooded**.
- The outside temperature changes a cold-blooded animal's body temperature.

Ask Questions

- What happens to insects as the temperature changes?
- How do insects move in different temperatures?

Make a Prediction

Here are two examples:

- Insects will move slowly when it is warm.
- Insects will move faster when it is warm.

Gather Your Supplies!

- Adult help
- Bug net
- A tall clear plastic cup
- A piece of mesh, 5 inches (13 cm) by 5 inches (13 cm)
- Clear tape
- Pencil or pen
- Paper
- Camera (optional)

Time to Experiment!

1. Grab your bug net and head outside! Bring your plastic cup and mesh with you.

2. Search for an insect. Have an adult help you. Some insects sting or bite! Check under rocks and logs. Look on trees and bushes. Ants, caterpillars, and moths are easy to find. Just pick one kind to study though.

3. Place your insect inside the plastic cup. Cover the cup with the mesh. Tape the sides of the mesh down over the lip of the cup.

4. Place the cup on the kitchen counter. Or find somewhere else inside your house that is not too cold.

5. Keep the plastic cup in its spot for about one hour. Check on the insect every 15 minutes. How is it acting? Is it moving a lot? Or is it staying pretty still? Write down what you notice on paper. Take photos or draw pictures, too.

6. At the end of one hour, move the cup to a cooler spot. Try the inside of your refrigerator.

7. Check on your insect every 15 minutes. Record anything you notice about the way it is acting.

8. At the end of one hour, bring your cup outside. Let your insect go.

Review the Results

Read your experiment notes. Study any photos you took or pictures you drew. How did the insect act in the warm and cold spots? The insect moved slowly in the cold. It moved faster in the warm temperature.

What Is Your Conclusion?

Did you predict the right answer? Temperature makes insects' muscles move in different ways. When it is warm, their muscles can move quickly. When it is cold, their muscles move slowly.

What are some other cold-blooded creatures? Spiders are also cold-blooded! Spiders are not insects though. They are animals called arachnids.

Same Bug, Different Shape

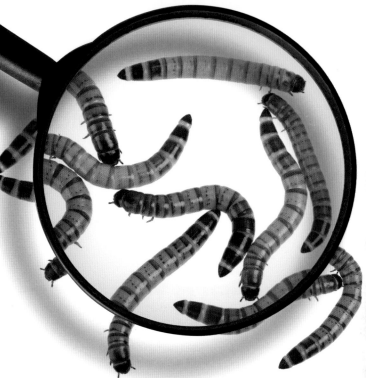

What changes happen during an insect's life cycle? See if an insect's body changes as it grows.

Research the Facts

Here are a few. What other facts can you find?

- Most insects change as they grow. They move from one stage to another.
- An insect's changes are its **metamorphosis**.

Ask Questions

- Do mealworms look different during their metamorphosis?
- What stages are in a mealworm's life cycle?

14

Make a Prediction

Here are two examples:

- Mealworms will have different shapes and forms as they grow.
- Mealworms look about the same during their lives.

Gather Your Supplies!

- Adult help
- A plastic container of mealworms (found at pet stores or bait shops)
- Uncooked oatmeal (a few tablespoons)
- Uncooked potato slices, about .25 inch (6.4 mm) thick
- Pencil or pen
- Paper
- Camera (optional)

Time to Experiment!

1. Place the oatmeal into your plastic container.
2. Have an adult cut the potato slice. Then drop it into the container.

3. How do the mealworms look now? Record what you observe. You can also draw pictures or take photos.
4. Keep the container on your kitchen counter. Feed the mealworms a new potato slice every few days.
5. At the end of one week, take a close look at the mealworms. Record what you notice. Do not forget to draw pictures or take photos!
6. Then bring your container outside. Let the mealworms go.

Mealworms shed their skins as they grow.

Review the Results

Study your notes. Look at any photos you took or pictures you drew. Did the mealworms change during the week? The mealworms' bodies should have changed in color and form.

What Is Your Conclusion?

What did you learn? Mealworms go through a metamorphosis. They start out with brown, hard bodies. As they grow, their bodies turn a light color. They also become soft and waxy. These changes are stages in their life cycle.

After a while, mealworms change again. They turn into black beetles!

Are houseflies social insects?

20

CHAPTER FIVE

Who Hangs with a Group?

How do different insects live? Find out if some live alone or in groups.

Research the Facts

Here are a few. What does your research show?

- Some insects are social. They live in groups.
- Other insects are **solitary**. They spend most of their time alone.

Ask Questions

- Which insects are social?
- Which insects are solitary?

Make a Prediction

Here are two examples:

- Ants are social. Flies are solitary.
- Both ants and flies are social.

Gather Your Supplies!

- Adult help
- Two types of insects (ants and flies)
- Pencil or pen
- Paper
- Camera (optional)

21

Time to Experiment!

1. You may want to ask an adult to help you. Watch out! Some insects sting or bite.

2. Look outside for ants. Check for anthills on the ground.

3. Once you find some ants, look at what they are doing. Do most move to and from the same area? Write down what you notice. You can also draw pictures or take photos.

4. Next search for flies. Look near garbage cans or around doors and windows.

5. Watch how the flies act. Do they all fly together? Or do they spend most of their time alone? Write down what you notice.

Review the Results

Look over your notes. Review any photos you took or pictures you drew. The ants were mostly in groups. The flies were mostly alone.

What Is Your Conclusion?

Was your prediction right? What did you learn about ants and flies? Ants are social insects. How about flies? Flies are solitary insects.

Most ants live in large groups. The groups are called colonies. A female ant is the queen. She leads the colony.

Crickets make noise with their legs.

24

CHAPTER SIX

Nighttime Noisemakers

Some insects make noise. Have you heard any on a summer night? Learn if darkness changes how much noise they make.

Research the Facts

Here are a few. What else do you know?

- Crickets chirp when they rub their wings together.
- Male crickets chirp to attract female crickets.

Ask Questions

- When do crickets chirp?
- Do crickets chirp more when it is dark or light out?

Make a Prediction

Here are two examples:

- Crickets chirp more when it is dark out.
- Crickets chirp only during the day.

Gather Your Supplies!

- A few crickets (found at pet stores)
- A tall clear plastic cup
- A piece of mesh, 5 inches (13 cm) by 5 inches (13 cm)
- Clear tape
- A small cardboard box
- A few pieces of newspaper
- Pencil or pen
- Paper
- A sound recorder (optional)

Time to Experiment!

1. Place the crickets inside your cup. Then cover the top with mesh. Tape the sides of the mesh down over the lip of the cup. Do this quickly! Crickets are fast jumpers!

2. Put the cup in a bright spot for about an hour. A counter near a window is a good place. Stay close to the cup. Listen carefully! Are the crickets chirping? How much? How loudly? Write down what you notice. Record their chirping with a sound recorder if you can.

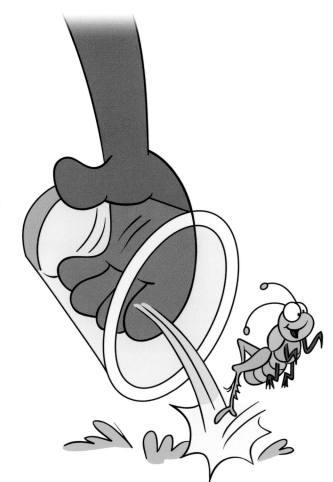

3. Next, move your cup inside the cardboard box. Cover the box opening with newspaper. Listen to their chirping for one hour. Write down what you notice. Or you can record their sounds.

4. Then go outside and set the crickets free.

Review the Results

Read your notes. Listen to the recordings you made. When did the crickets chirp more? The crickets chirped less by the window. The crickets chirped more in the cardboard box.

What Is Your Conclusion?

Were you right? Crickets chirp more when it is dark. Animals that eat crickets move more during the day. It is safer for crickets to be noisy at night.

Crickets also chirp more when it is warmer outside. This is because they are cold-blooded. They are more active when the temperature is higher.

You are a scientist now. What fun insect facts did you learn? You found out that insects are cold-blooded. You saw that their bodies change form and shape as they grow. You can learn even more about insects. Study them. Experiment with them. Then share what you learn about insects.

Glossary

abdomen (AB-duh-muhn): The abdomen is the rear section of an insect's body. The abdomen is one of the three insect body parts.

arachnids (ah-RACH-nidz): Arachnids are a type of animal with an exoskeleton and eight legs. Spiders are arachnids.

cold-blooded (KOLD-BLUHD-id): A cold-blooded animal has a body that changes temperature when the temperature around it changes. Insects are cold-blooded.

conclusion (kuhn-KLOO-shuhn): A conclusion is what you learn from doing an experiment. The experiment's conclusion was that crickets move more in the heat.

exoskeleton (eks-oh-SKEL-uht-uhn): An exoskeleton is the bony covering of an animal's body. An ant has an exoskeleton.

experiment (ek-SPER-uh-ment): An experiment is a test or way to study something to learn facts. The experiment tested a question about flies.

metamorphosis (met-uh-MOR-fuh-siss): Metamorphosis is the series of changes some animals go through between hatching and adulthood. A caterpillar goes through a metamorphosis.

prediction (pri-DIKT-shun): A prediction is what you think will happen in the future. The prediction about the experiment with worms was right.

social (SO-shuhl): Social animals live in groups, not alone. Some ants are social insects.

solitary (SOL-uh-ter-ee): Solitary animals live alone, not in groups. Insects can be solitary.

thorax (THOR-aks): A thorax is the middle section of an insect's body. An insect's legs connect to its thorax.

Books

Trueit, Trudi Strain. *Ants*. New York: Marshall Cavendish Benchmark, 2010.

Woodward, John. *Cricket: Garden Minibeasts Up Close*. New York: Chelsea Clubhouse, 2010.

Young, Karen Romano. *Bug Science: Twenty Projects and Experiments about Arthropods: Insects, Arachnids, Algae, Worms, and Other Small Creatures*. Washington, D.C.: National Geographic, 2009.

Web Sites

Visit our Web site for links about insect experiments:
childsworld.com/links

Note to Parents, Teachers, and Librarians: We routinely verify our Web links to make sure they are safe and active sites. So encourage your readers to check them out!

ABOUT THE AUTHOR:
Katie Marsico has written more than 80 books for children and young adults. She lives in Elmhurst, Illinois, with her husband and children.